Making Roads

Written by Ratu Mataira

Roads help people go
from place to place.
There are many kinds
of roads.
Look at all
the different roads.

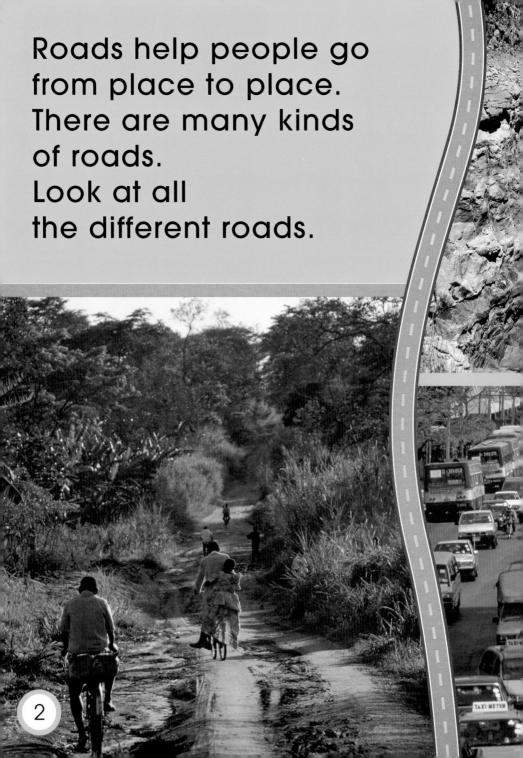

These people
are making a new road.
They will take away
the trees.

They will take away
stones and dirt, too.
This can be
very hard work.

People making a new road.

But trucks and bulldozers can help. They can do the work for people.

Some other machines can help make the road, too.

truck

bulldozer

7

Trucks put sand
and stone
on the road.

Graders make
the road flat.

Rollers make
the road hard.

Other machines
put down the tar.

truck

grader

roller

tar sealer

These people are making
a new road.
They are making it
out of concrete.

Look at the cranes.

The cranes help put
the concrete
into place.

The new road will be
a highway.

crane

When a road comes
to the water,
a bridge can be made.

A lot of bridges are
made out of steel.

A boat comes with
steel on it.

A crane takes
the steel
up to the bridge.

new bridge

boat

crane

13

Now the new road goes
over the water.
People can go from
one place to the other!

Index

Guide Notes

Title: Making Roads
Stage: Early (3) – Blue

Genre: Nonfiction
Approach: Guided Reading
Processes: Thinking Critically, Exploring Language, Processing Information
Written and Visual Focus: Photographs (static images), Index, Labels, Caption
Word Count: 180

THINKING CRITICALLY
(sample questions)
- Look at the front cover and the title. Ask the children what they know about making roads.
- Look at the title and read it to the children.
- Focus the children's attention on the index. Ask: "What are you going to find out about in this book?"
- If you want to find out about making roads with machines, which pages would you look on?
- If you want to find out about making a highway, which page would you look on?
- Look at pages 4 and 5. Why do you think so many people are needed to make the new road?
- Look at pages 12 and 13. Why do you think a crane is needed to lift up the steel?

EXPLORING LANGUAGE

Terminology
Title, cover, photographs, author, photographers

Vocabulary
Interest words: trucks, bulldozers, machines, graders, rollers, tar, concrete, highway, cranes, steel
High-frequency words: many, making, other, new
Positional words: on, down, up, into, over
Compound words: highway, into

Print Conventions
Capital letter for sentence beginnings, periods, commas, exclamation mark